Anonymous

Memorial of Kate Benedict Freeman

Anonymous

Memorial of Kate Benedict Freeman

ISBN/EAN: 9783337278694

Printed in Europe, USA, Canada, Australia, Japan

Cover: Foto ©Raphael Reischuk / pixelio.de

More available books at **www.hansebooks.com**

OF

KATE BENEDICT FREEMAN.

𝔓𝔯𝔦𝔫𝔱𝔢𝔡 𝔣𝔬𝔯 𝔓𝔯𝔦𝔟𝔞𝔱𝔢 𝔠𝔦𝔯𝔠𝔲𝔩𝔞𝔱𝔦𝔬𝔫.

NEW YORK:

ROBERT CARTER AND BROTHERS,

530, BROADWAY.

1870.

"SHE liveth long who liveth well:
  All other life is short and vain;
She liveth longest who can tell
  Of living most for heavenly gain.

" She liveth long who liveth well!
  All else is being flung away;
She liveth longest who can tell
  Of true things truly done each day."

BONAR.

I.

THE SCHOOL-GIRL.

"GOOD lives are like rays of sunlight, that gladden the world
while they shine, but leave it dark
and chilly when they depart. Feeble
and faint at best must be the image
of a life transferred to a printed page,
in comparison with that life itself, as
it was felt by friends while it lasted,
and is remembered still; but if the
original were indeed a sunbeam sent
from heaven to cheer a portion of
this dull earth, a copy, to some extent
true and suggestive, may be taken
and kept."

This little Memorial lays no claim to being a biography, but aims merely to give a brief outline of the dear departed one, to help friends more vividly to recall the vanished life.

Kate Benedict was born in the city of New York, on the 19th of May, 1841.

As a child she was remarkable for her vivacity and wit, and for the zest with which she entered into both her employments and enjoyments.

Her education was mainly acquired at the Spingler Institute, under the kind care of the Rev. Gorham D. Abbott.

One of her teachers writes: "I remember her perfectly, and her distinguishing traits of character; affectionate, talented, studious, bright, susceptible always to the highest motives. If I wished to move her to a certain course of action, which perhaps was new and strange to her, I had merely to appeal to her sense of right. and a conscience evidently educated by the word of God would invariably respond to my call. Her temperament was peculiarly cheerful, kind, and genial, and she was therefore a universal favorite with her teachers. and also her associates. She won easily, and retained the love of all.

" As I write, one characteristic occurs to me, which illustrates her cheerfulness as well as her kindness of heart. She loved sport, — a play upon words. or an innocent joke, — but would never go so far as to wound the feelings of any. On the contrary,

I remember she would be among the first to cheer a schoolmate who was depressed, or incite her to renewed study so as to avoid censure; or, as in one case particularly before my mind, bring them to me repentant, and go away with the forgiven one apparently as happy as if she herself had been forgiven."

One of her classmates writes as follows: —

" I well remember the first time that Katie's bright, good-natured face appeared in our school-room; and from that day until we finished the prescribed course of study, five years afterwards, she was truly *the life of the class.* In the times of intermission, there was always a laughing group of girls gathered about her,

enjoying her funny sayings. In fact,
we grew to expect 'fun' as a matter
of course, when Kate was present,
and she seldom failed to respond to
our desire. Add to her readiness of
speech a great facility with her pen-
cil, and you will perceive that she
was a treasure to us.

"Under this joyous exterior Kate
treasured deep, even enthusiastic, feelings on many subjects.

"At that time her religious senti-
ments were mostly shut up within
her own heart, — not a subject of conversation with others.

"She was exceedingly fond of the
study of history, not as a school-study,
but for her own home reading; and
often as we sat together painting, with
our easels side by side, would she

express her admiration for certain historical personages. I remember her once saying to me that she would rather have been Mme. Roland than any other historical personage she knew of. Her sympathy with the noble, self-sacrificing spirit of that unfortunate lady will perhaps show some of her own characteristics."

During this period she was presented by her father with a neat little gold watch, which she greatly valued, not only for its own sake, but also for the sake of the giver. But of course she had to take it to Spingler to show to her schoolmates. After returning from school one afternoon, she missed it. Diligent search was at once made, but all in vain. Though then perhaps not a Christian,

yet she knew well the power of prayer;
for she dwelt in a household where
prayer was much valued. So she
took her trouble to the Lord. She
prayed that He who knew all things
would point out to her where her
watch was. She followed up these
petitions with fresh efforts in the way
of search, but still no clew could be
found to the missing article. Before
retiring to rest for the night. she once
more committed the matter to the
Lord, and again on rising in the morning. She started for school at the
usual time, and as she passed down
to the street from the front door, on
the lowest step, fast embedded in the
ice, lay her lost treasure. It certainly seemed a remarkable answer to
prayer; for both in the evening and

again in the morning, a great many had passed up and down that thoroughfare (Madison Avenue), but their eyes had been holden so that they should not see what really lay so conspicuously before them.

In this little incident we have the key to her subsequent success in the service of the Master. Whenever any trouble arose, she went and told Jesus. When she was in doubt or difficulty, she took both doubts and difficulties to Him. The extracts from her letters and journal in this little Memorial show this, and her life exemplified it still more conspicuously.

Her attainments at school, without being marked, were highly satisfactory.

There have been preserved twenty

of her compositions, neatly folded, and tied up with a pink ribbon. These show more facility in expression and more vigor of thought than is usually found in the writings of girls at her age.

While at school, the summer months were always spent at Lake Mahopac, N.Y.

Here she was the leader in every innocent frolic, such as making molasses candy, picking blackberries, enjoying a straw ride, or rowing, as the case might be.

Here that remarkable unselfishness, afterwards so conspicuous a trait in her character, began to develop itself. She was the universal favorite among all the girls, — for it was the companionship of her own sex only that she sought.

No letters of this period have been preserved to throw light on her character and employments. But all who knew her think of her as a warm-hearted, loving, witty, clever girl; somewhat of a romp, perhaps, but a romp that never hurt any one's feelings, and was always doing kind things to others.

II.

THE YOUNG WOMAN.

ON the first Sabbath in April, 1858, Kate united with the Madison-square Presbyterian Church (Rev. Dr. Adams's). Her Christian character is well expressed by the words of Scripture, " The path of the just is as the shining light that shineth more and more unto the perfect day." Its great characteristic was *growth*. That growth was particularly marked and rapid in the last year of her life.

In 1864 her father removed to Audubon Park, 155th Street. Here she and other members of the family united with the Presbyterian Church under the pastoral care of the Rev. C. A. Stoddard. A strong bond of attachment soon sprang up between the pastor and this loving parishioner. There was here an ample field for Christian labor. She became immediately an earnest worker in the Sabbath school.

Twice a month she invited her scholars to her house, and gave them a little entertainment as well as read to them. It is remembered that on one occasion, finding that four of her scholars wanted very much to see the panorama of Bunyan's Pilgrim's Progress, then exhibiting in Dr. Cheever's church, with no little self-denial she took them all with her to see it.

Again, hearing that two of the little girls had never seen Broadway or Stewart's store, she took them by stage (a kind of conveyance they had never travelled in before) down Broadway, and carefully showed them all the wonders of Stewart's, as well as took them to the Egyptian museum at that time on exhibition.

One case of a very sick woman is now vividly recalled, whom she visited every day, and sometimes twice, carrying always some delicacy suited to her feeble condition and flagging appetite. In fact she took upon herself nearly the whole care of this woman, and was with her when she died.

At the funeral she led the little children by the hand, and followed the coffin as chief mourner to the grave.

About the death of this woman she writes, April 9th, 1865: —

" Poor Mrs. —— died Wednesday morning; *so* gently, *so* calmly, as if going to sleep. Just before she passed away she opened her eyes, a sweet smile came over her face, she stretched out her arms, and joyfully whispering, ' *Happy, happy,*' was gone. I felt so unhappy before: I could not rid myself of the terrible thought I was answerable for the indifference (if such it was), — I could not help but recall neglected opportunities. But now I am sure she is with Jesus. Why did those eyes unclose, and the smile come over those wasted features, unless they had seen that blessed face looking down in love and forgiveness? What could make her stretch out those poor thin arms, and exultingly cry, 'Happy, happy,' when the dark river was yet to be crossed alone? *Alone !* ah, no! she saw the Saviour's arms outstretched to receive her, and hastened to meet Him. Folded in that loving embrace, with her head pillowed on His bosom, she can utter words of joy. Safely now the dark river is crossed,—its waters did not overflow her; up, up to the pearly gates of heaven she is borne. and as they open wide to receive her, there the white-robed ones are waiting to welcome 'mother,' united never to part again. There at the feet of the Saviour may it be she has found that *Rest* which only He can give."

It was proposed some time since to enter more earnestly on the work of tract distribution, and the Church called for volunteers to visit in certain peculiarly difficult districts. Kate came forward at once and offered her services. Hers was one of the hardest to do, because she had to distribute them among her own friends.

She never went down town without taking a few little books or tracts with her, to give to such children as she might meet on the way.

One striking peculiarity was her thoughtfulness about others, — her desire to do kind things to those who might be overlooked, or those who had few friends.

On one occasion, for instance, she sent a kind letter to a dress-maker, who had worked for her, accompanied by Dr. Hall's admirable little book, "Care Cast upon the Lord." On being spoken to about it, she remarked that a dress-maker's life must be so full of trials and cares that she thought this little book would be a comfort to her.

Calling one day on a neighbor, she learned through a little child in the family that the grandmother's birthday would be in a few days. Kate said nothing about it at the time, but when the day arrived, thinking that the excellent old lady would perhaps have no one to remember the day, outside of her own family, sent her a pot of full-blown roses, charging the bearer not to tell who sent them.

A few days after, she met the lady's daughter in the car, on the way to New York. The latter, not sus-

pecting Kate's connection with the
matter, spoke of the flowers her mother had received on her birthday,
and how happy they had made her.
Kate, without thought, exclaimed, —
" I am so glad she liked them! " and
then added, " Oh, I did not mean to
tell, but please say nothing to your
mother about it." Her wishes were
respected, and the aged servant of
Christ knew nothing about the giver
till after Kate's death.

When the war broke out, " she used
to tell me," says a schoolmate, from
whose letter we have already made
quotations, " of her desire to make
herself useful as a nurse to the wounded soldiers in hospital; and although
the plan was not carried out, she kept
up her interest in them, and she re-

counted to me the pleasure it gave
her to distribute magazines to them,
or to leave a few choice flowers by
the pillow of a sleeping soldier, so
that their beauty and fragrance might
cheer him when he awoke."

Twice or three times every week
she visited the soldiers' hospital, at
Central Park. She carried them jel-
lies and other tempting viands, as
well as books, tracts, and flowers;
and, what was perhaps best of all,
gave them many loving words of
sympathy and encouragement.

Afterwards she received several
letters from the convalescents.

One of these poor fellows, in a
cramped hand, the words badly
spelled, and with little regard to gram-
mar, says: " I am writing to express

the warm thanks I feel. You do not know the pleasure that them flowers you gave me produced. I smell them now, and likewise the books that you gave me. I hope that you may get your reward in heaven. You are the soldier's friend. When you came in the ward and gave out these flowers and then said you was sorry you had no more left, you gave me one and smiled so pleasantly."

Another one sent his photograph, and says: "There is nothing that will comfort a soldier so much as kind words from a lady. I am happy to say that I am a soldier of the cross, as well as a soldier in this war. I may soon be on my way to the front, to stand my chance once more in the thinned ranks, where once stood a thousand strong. If I go and don't have the pleasure of seeing you, please remember me in your prayers."

Many a poor home was made brighter by her friendly visits; many a little want supplied; many a loving word spoken for the Master, for whose sake she did it all.

She took great delight in hanging up on the walls of the houses of the poor, and especially of the sick poor, copies of the " Silent Comforter," which consists of large-type Scripture texts, and hymns.

In her attention to her duties as a servant of the Lord Jesus, she did not overlook that intellectual culture which became one in her position and with her opportunities. She acquired great skill in drawing and painting,

as the walls, alike of her first home
and her last one, attest. She also
contributed some interesting articles
to one of the religious newspapers.
Extracts from letters of this period
follow, illustrative of her Christian
character. These letters evince a
remarkable devotion to duty. When
the question was once settled what
she *ought* to do, she lost no time in
setting about it. She was one of the
most gifted of letter-writers. It is
greatly to be regretted that that spark-
ling wit with which they overflowed
was generally of such a strictly personal or private nature as to forbid
their being printed. It must not be
supposed that because these extracts
are largely of a serious character that
there was any thing sad, morbid, or

melancholy in her religion. On the
contrary, she was, both in conversation and correspondence, as all who
knew her will testify, one of the live-
liest, wittiest, and most entertaining
of persons.

Her letters were many of them not
only of the most amusing sort, but
they were often illustrated with pen-
sketches of inimitable drollery.

In May, 1866, her father, having
occasion to go to St. Louis to attend
the General Assembly, took Kate with
him to Niagara Falls, and after spend-
ing some time there, took her to a
friend's house in Western Canada
(now Ontario), where he left her till
his return.

In a letter to her mother she gives
some of her experience in a sleeping-
car, on the outward trip: —

"While we were quietly sitting by our window the man put his head in: 'Want your bed made, sir?' Up we jumped, going out into the dressing-room, to wait until it was ready. I watched the mysterious proceedings, — tumbling down shelves, dragging out sheets, tossing up pillows, and all prepared in about two minutes. I looked with a little trepidation at the size of the room after the bed was made. It was all bed from window to door, and from wall to wall. I lay down on the outside, entirely dressed except my hat; put something between my head and the pillow, and wondered would I ever sleep in that place. . . .

"I lay staring awake; I could hear the wheels scratching and groaning, and hear the shriek, and feel the jerk, clickety click, sic, sic, sic, blickety blick. bic. clic. clic, clic; and then faster, — blickelty blick, blickelty, blickelty, blickelty. until I wanted to scream. Somehow I did fall asleep, though when I cannot conceive; but I jumped up at every station, and heard the voices outside and baggage put off, and the train move on. It must have been near two o'clock, when I felt this could be endured no longer. I sat up in bed and thought. I remembered they were all asleep in that whole train. I began to think every thing was asleep in the world, — that the world had stopped moving, — that the engineer was asleep too, and the train was rushing off to destruction. For a moment the

thought was horrible. I wanted to
bang on the door and wake every
one up. Then I suddenly recollected
the robber was to come for my rings,
and he ought to be along soon, for it
was going on to morning. I put
them on the end of my thumb, so
they might be conveniently stolen
without sawing off my fingers,—raised
up my chin that he might see my
breast-pin, without hacking off my
head, — and waited. He was asleep,
too! Thank his blessed bed for that.
I felt cheered; and, in that sweet reflection, fell asleep."

To Mr. Freeman she writes of the
following day's travel: —

"The journey the next day was perfectly delightful. Such a beautiful
country, so open, so wild, and so

charmingly picturesque. The motion
of travelling was so even and smooth
that we glided rather than rushed
past the fields and fences. Now we
would be hanging over a very great
height, where right below lay a lovely
lake sweetly sunny, and reflecting the
sky above us in its clear blue surface;
then, speeding past the thick, dark
wood, little openings now and then
showed us the wood-slides cut in the
mountain-side; now a quick curve
into a lovely table-land, stretching
far, far away, and all a bright golden
green. Only for a moment, though;
for with a shriek and a snort, our wild
horse rushes past a wooden house,
making me involuntarily draw back,
frightened lest the man at the window
might suffer. But I look back, and

see him smiling and tossing his hat in
welcome, all safe. Here we leave a
barn, almost destroyed, when hurrah!
we find it again, as if godmother fairies
had granted the annual boon: oh, it
was glorious, this mad flight through
the air! And then to go slower, slower,
slower; to hear the pant and puff, to
feel the motion, gentler, gentler, and to
see the train move into the rural depot,
where would be crouching in comfort
on rude settles the weather-browned
fathers of the land, wonderingly ey-
ing us travellers from the great
'York.' How I enjoyed it! I have
thanked my father, who so continually
added each moment to my comfort
and enjoyment. But *our* Father in
Heaven I cannot thank enough for so
much happiness, and such a profusion

of blessings. I am brought after every mercy nearer to Him. I feel my own sinfulness and utter unworthiness to receive these privileges. Oh! then may I live more devotedly for His service, and serve only for His glory."

In the same letter she gives her impressions of Niagara Falls, which she saw now for the first and only time : —

"I cannot tell you how the Falls affected me. They are so awful, horrible, maddening, the tremendous fall of waters! Nothing I ever conceived is like it. The rapids where the water is howling, shrieking, dashing over the rocks, rolling up in great billows to break in the air, or to leap into another, and then struggling together, go down, down, down that frightful fall. As I watched them and listened to the awful roar, I felt perfectly fascinated. I wanted to plunge in, that I might feel the great mystery. Then my knees trembled so that I sank down, crying and calling to father to come and save me. Father was so good, and kept his arm around me all the while. With him to hold me, I could look up and admire the dizzy height? but my feeble knees tottered even then, and I only breathed freely when we were up the long stairway again, away from the roar and whirl. It seemed like Hell, and the rapids like those struggling to get free, but too late whirled down to destruction, and the eternal volume of waters and horrible roar, like an avenging God. I could not think

of Him as the same sweet and loving
Jesus I wanted to please and live
for."

"The next day I went again with
father to see the Falls in the sunlight.
They were too bewilderingly, glori-
ously magnificent for me to describe:
the changing color,—the soft white
spray, — the swift, steep fall of water.
God grant you to see it all, and to wonder at the might of our Father's power
to command the waves and winds to
obey Him! The rapids! Oh, how
they would delight you! How they
danced, shouted, roared, laughed, and
frolicked in the greatest glee; rising
high in air to scatter spray mischiev-
ously, wanting to make us feel their
furious power; crashing over rocks,
striking into one another, madly strug-

gling in the air, then rushing different ways to foam and boil the water everywhere. Then to look 'way up the lake, as far as the eye could reach, and to see the rapids there higher in air, showing the gradual descent of water, and clearly demonstrating the cause of the terrible rush of all that great gathering into one stupendous descent."

Under date of May 16, to Mr. Freeman, she says: —

"And now I am in Canada, the land of old John Bull. No *Britainer am I, though!* American from head to foot; *loyal*, too, to the very core! And a strange life I am living among the queer old Canadian farmers. Not half-and-half farmers, but real, true farmers: clean, though; every thing scrupulously neat, from the kitchen floor to the old man's cow-byre."

"Yesterday afternoon I went to a *neighbor's* — a mile and a half away — to spend the afternoon and take tea. I had a splendid time. It is a real farm family; even the father has never been to *New York!* But they were all so hospitable and intelligent, and treated me elegantly. Just imagine, they have a melodeon, and one of the daughters takes lessons in singing! Of course, I played, and they were delighted, imagining I must be *Signor La Pokèc!!* There was a crazy-looking man staying there, a singing-master, and such a funny man he was too. He was one of that kind who, when they sit down, seem to melt into the legs of the chair, and you

wonder where they have gone to. I
don't know what he thought, but he
laughed at every word I said, and
seemed to enjoy 'the New-York lady'
very much. It is a great thing to
come from 'the States;' and here they
think you something wonderful if
they hear you are from 'New York.'
There was to be a concert in the
'Hall' at Mount Hope, about three
miles from their house. Of course I
must go everywhere, so off we went,
in a pouring rain too. But I did not
get wet, for it was a covered wagon,
and my lovely singing-master drove
the '*team*.' Over bridges and brooks
we went, until we drove into a mite
of a village, and up to the hall. How
they stared at me! I could see the
young men nudging one another to

know who I was, and then the staring
would go on fiercer than ever. The
concert began very shortly after we
had our seats in this queer 'hall,' and
do you believe it was only *three
men*, who sang quartets, triplets, and
duets all together? But they did
have elegant, deep voices, only they
made up such funny faces, as if they
smelt something very peculiar."

Three days later she thus describes
a scene in the Canadian woods in a
letter to Mr. Freeman:—

"Oh! it is so perfectly beautiful
out in the wild woods where I am
now. I cannot describe to you the
charming spot we have chosen in
which to spend the day. *It is too
exquisitely beautiful.* I am sitting on
a fallen tree, close by the water.

Very near me is a ruined saw-mill,
with the logs and beams heaped together in most picturesque confusion.
I cannot see a house or the faintest
sign of any habitation. It is all wild-
wood and green meadow-land; bright
green: *oh, such a lovely green!* The
trees are not so densely foliaged but
that I can look beyond to broader
fields and deeper woods and sunnier
meadows than even this seems to be.
The birds are singing loudly in the
branches overhead. I can hear the
squirrels, and see them besides, as
they run to and fro. And now I hear
the tinkling of bells. *How very
rural!* I look up and see four cows
coming down to drink from my sweet
little brook. Our dog 'Help' sitting
beside us watches them for a moment;

and then springing up, dashes over
the water, plunges into a thicket, and
is gone! 'He has seen something,'
Marie says. Sure enough, with a
wild cry, a flock of birds rise in the
air, wheel in circles for an instant,
and then sweep away in the distance.
Back comes the rude invader, shakes
off the water in our very faces,
crouches down into the most comfortable position, and now lazily
closes his eyes, pretending to be very
innocent. Oh, how I love it! This
place is so beautiful, and yet so
grandly wild. It is *all God everywhere.* Man has not placed his hand
here. God speaks in this very still-
ness, and shows me the worthlessness
of man's invention compared to His
own glorious works. It is just the

beautiful scenery that would charm you. I think if we were here together now, we would know better how to praise the God who formed us, and allows us, even for a season, to enjoy the delight of living in such a beautiful world, — a world defiled only by sin, but which if peopled by angels would be almost heaven."

To her little sister during the same visit she writes: —

". . . They have five cows, and I go out to see them milked. Sometimes they almost kick the pail over, and throw their tails around so funnily. And they have such lovely ducks, that say 'gabble, gabble,' all day. And such a big dog, named Help. I was afraid of him when I first came, he looked so fierce: I thought he would eat all my bones. Now I am getting used to him, and I don't mind at all when he crawls under the table at dinner time and lies down at my feet. There is another dog, too, but he is a dear *little* one named Judy. I am not afraid of him. One day I saw such a large pig in the road, and what do you think? There were seven little mites of pigs running after her. They looked so funny with their short tails just about as long as your little finger, all wriggling in the air; and you don't know how they squealed as they ran after their mother. I think they must have loved her dearly; but I am afraid she hadn't punished them enough, they were so rude and un-gentlemanly to make such a loud noise.

"Oh! I must tell you something else. Marie has the loveliest pet lamb, named Abraham Lincoln. Jessie has another, named Jefferson Davis. They are so sweet, and as white as snow. We go in the fields where they are, and the moment they see us coming, down they will scamper to meet us. Wasn't it too bad, Jessie sold her lamb to the butcher? She wanted to keep him very much; but then you know the money would do her a great deal more good, and the butcher gave her two dollars and a half for it. You must ask Georgie to tell you how many pennies this is. I suppose the dear little lamb had his cunning white head taken off yesterday, and somebody may eat him by and by. He had an ugly name, didn't he? — Jeff Davis.

"Marie says she will not sell hers; so it is very nice to think that I am to have Abraham Lincoln for my friend while I am in Canada: isn't it? I have seen Johnnie Grey and Jessie Grey and Bessie Grey and Charlie Grey. Jessie Grey is just like a little boy. She can climb fences and run on stone walls and do all sorts of wild things, and she is only four years old! She says my name is Miss Benk-kit. Isn't that a funny name for me?

"When I was there yesterday she had a little gray pussy in her arms. If it scratches her she rolls it up in the bedclothes and lays it in the cradle. Then she rocks the cradle so fast that, between the bedclothes and the rocking, the poor puss almost

smothers. I think it must be very
glad when Bessie's mamma puts her
little girl to bed for the night: don't
you? Charlie is the baby, so he does
nothing but crow and kick his feet
all day long.

I miss you very much, darling; but
then I try not to, for God is very good
to make me so happy: isn't he? Are
you trying to be good, dear, too?
You mustn't forget what I told you
about your prayers. Remember not
to pray for to-morrow; only to ask
God to make you a good little girl
for to-day. Then to-night you must
think what you have done naughty,
and ask Jesus to forgive it all. Afterwards pray Him to watch you safely
through the night, and to-morrow ask
Jesus to love and keep you through

the day. Isn't that a nicer way than to say such long prayers? for Jesus would rather have us tell Him all what we do naughty, and what we want good: then He can give us all we need to make us good Christian children. Be kind to Georgie: won't you, darling pet? Remember Jesus is looking at you all the while, and every time you please Him you make that naughty Satan go away from your heart, and the dear Jesus comes in. Be kind to Matilda too. You know poor Matilda's mother lives far away in Germany. You would feel lonely sometimes if your mother lived there: wouldn't you? So be kind to her, and Jesus will love you very dearly if you do every thing just because you want to show Him how dearly you love Him."

To a dear sister at school she thus writes, May 14, 1866, from Audubon Park: —

"I pray God to keep you well, happy, and full of His sweet Spirit, so that every one in school will love you, and see that you love Jesus."

The following words of encouragement are addressed to the same sister in July: —

" I notice so many times lately that you have given up your own will to please others. Jesus has said, ' If any man love me let him deny himself, and take up his cross and follow me.' You may be sure then that you do love Jesus when you deny yourself, and are willing to suffer little annoyances for His sake. . . . So you will keep on exerting a good influence:

won't you, dear sister? Don't be
discouraged if you can't see any good
done. Remember Jesus has said,
'Whatsoever ye ask, believing, you
shall receive.' He doesn't say right
away now. We must believe it will
come some time."

In July, 1866, she spent two weeks
with her sister and brother-in-law at
Stockbridge, Mass. She thus describes her experience in the boat for
Albany: —

"Our state-room was in the centre
of the boat (the St. John), very comfortable and every thing convenient.
Mr. Carter's was next, so that made
us feel almost at home. Of course
we were so anxious to catch the first
glimpse of Audubon, that our eyes
hurried over other objects. At last

we saw the Iron Foundry, the River House, and then home. But oh we were so disappointed! You didn't seem to be there at all. It looked like so many croquet sticks. I mean black winning-posts. I only recognized one, and that was little Jessie. . . . I saw father dip the flag, or rather just saw the flag dipped, — we could not recognize any one. Emma, not feeling very well, went to her room early. Mr. Carter made a sweet little prayer with her before she went to sleep; and then he and I, like two grave married folks, sat on deck, peering out into the dark waters. We noticed every point of interest, St. Anthony's Nose, Cro' Nest, West Point, and oh so many magnificent high peaks, almost mountains, close to the water's edge! We sat on deck till it was near ten o'clock: another prayer was said for me as we knelt down together in the little state-room, and then we separated for the night. I had been in that cramped-up place but a few moments, when Emma awoke. She felt a great deal better.

"The window in our room looked out on something, we puzzled our heads to find out *what*. It looked like a long counter. . . . I felt very nervous. I thought of the sign reiterated on every column in the saloon, ' Beware of strangers handsomely dressed who invite you to play euchre.' I could see the long counter just outside, and, in imagination, the handsomely dressed stranger stretched upon it gazing in at us. 'Emma,' I asked, 'suppose that man comes and asks us to play, what will you do?' 'Oh!' she said, 'play of course,' and then we both laughed."

Ten days later she writes to her father from Stockbridge: —

"I know I am coming home in two or three days, but nevertheless I must write you a few little lines. We have had a delightful visit. Mr. Carter and Mary have taken us everywhere, I should think, and yet they are continually proposing new excursions. We walk and ride a part of every day, and are getting so thoroughly acclimated that one would suppose, from our healthy countenances and hearty appreciation of the Berkshire hills, we were children of the soil.

Not only have we become interested in Stockbridge, but also in Lenox and Great Barrington. We thought Lenox lovely, and the view from the Aspinwall place grander than any I have seen. I should say *more beautiful,*—for the valley below and distant mountains are seen distinctly here; whereas, at Mount Washington and Catskill, it is their indistinctness, and the great extent of country, far, far below and around you, that makes the view so grand.

"Great Barrington we visited yesterday. The drive out was delightful, by the Housatonic River the entire way. I did not go into raptures, though; for the track was close at our side, the cars were expected in a little time, and our horse was terribly afraid of the locomotive. However, fast driving brought us into Great Barrington before the appearance of the dreaded train.

"We had to leave in a pretty heavy shower, in order to reach Stockbridge in time for tea; but we had waterproof cloaks, so we drove home in fine condition. It was a much pleasanter ride back, because we left the railway altogether, coming over Monument Mountain.

"Sunday morning we attended church in Stockbridge village. It is a very large building, and well filled by the 'old families.'

"I saw the Rev. Dr. Field there; and he looked so finely, with that beautiful silver hair so smoothly falling on his shoulders.

"It was through one of the members of the Field family that Mr. Carter heard, after church, of the success of the Atlantic Cable. I could imagine the joy such an event must produce throughout all England and America; and I could imagine too how delightedly you, dear father, must have read the thrilling despatch that the cable was laid, and how earnestly you thanked God in prayer, and desired that it might continue a success and a blessing to the world.

"I wish I could give you a good description of the graveyard we went through in Stockbridge. I can only give you a faint one, for all such places must be seen in order to be perfectly appreciated. It is very prettily and neatly laid out, just as every thing is in Massachusetts. There are many plain white monuments reared to commemorate our Revolutionary Fathers, and by their side newer graves and fresher slabs to honor the younger brave of the Massachusetts 49th. So side by side '76 and '61 rest together.

"What interested me most was the Sedgwick burying-ground. This is portioned off entirely from the other part. In the centre is a large column to the memory of the father, while clustered round it are the children and grandchildren. There was one very pretty grave: the head-piece was a brown-stone cross, and around the centre part a plain belt of the same stone with just the name 'Helen,' while at the foot was a brown-stone dog beautifully carved, and sitting just as if in life. On the collar was the name 'Grip.' It seems the dog loved little Helen very dearly. It was such a pretty idea, and made the tears come when looking at it.

"Right in among the family names was a bright white stone, and on it 'Elizabeth Freeman, known as Mum-Bet.' And then it said that she had been for thirty years of her life an African slave, — that she had never neglected a duty, never violated a trust. Such a beautiful eulogy to the Christian life of that bondwoman, that I almost envied her such a life. It seemed as if her life should be a lesson to us, that if an African slave could be such a Christian, how much must God expect from us living under such different circumstances."

A highly cultivated lady, the wife of a Presbyterian clergyman, in northern Illinois, who was very intimate with Kate, writes thus, under date of March 20, 1870: —

"On my last visit to her father's house, a sympathy sprang up between us from the fact that she was expecting to assume the responsibilities of a pastor's wife. We talked over its blessings, its duties, and its trials. She expressed an entire willingness to leave her delightful, happy home, and work for Jesus anywhere.

"The last morning I spent in that beautiful home, the bell rang for prayers. (Her father had been called away the day previous on business.) As I entered the dining-room, I found the family all assembled (fifteen of

us), including the servants and coachman, and dear Kate in her father's
accustomed seat, with the Bible, from
which she read a chapter, and then
knelt and offered up a prayer, so full
of love, so appropriate to each of our
cases, so full of trust and confidence
in the precious promises of God, that
I could not but admire the noble girl
whose piety shone so brightly. None
could help feeling that she had been
with Jesus, and learned of Him."

This was not a solitary instance of
taking her father's place in his ab-
sence, but her constant habit, through
many years.

The following letter from Kate was
addressed to this excellent lady, under
date of Dec. 14th, 1866: —

"Father is very well, and just as

strongly pre-millennial as ever. Of course we have the benefit of his careful researches at morning prayers. Sometimes it is about 'going up,' or the rapid decline of the Papal power. Yesterday morning he told us that the Pope had gone to some place, I forget the name; and father spoke so excitedly of the horrors of such a system, that the coachman rolled his eyes around wildly, and squeezed his chair close to the wall, as if he feared the Pope might cram in behind him.

"No matter what horrible event might occur, it would be to father nothing but a glorious fulfilment of the prophecies. But he is such a good man, such a darling father, and such a perfectly beautiful Christian, that everybody loves him, even our old cat.

"He has taken up (father. — not the 'old cat'*) Revelation now, as a study in his Bible class; the expositions are certainly most thrillingly interesting: every verse seems to speak for itself. . . .

"I could not help loving that good man, your husband, when I heard you relate those stories of hospital life, and what he did to relieve the suffering of the poor soldiers. . . . Give him the books I send. I would like to send him a whole library full. I know the little I do give will be

---

* This parenthesis is not so unnecessary as a stranger might suppose; for Dr. Faustus, as this great, wise, and companionable household favorite was called, was no ordinary cat. He lived to extreme old age, and his portrait, life-size, painted by Kate's skilful hand, remains to commemorate his virtues.

blessed to him, as I give it from love to Jesus; and given with that love in the heart to one whose sole aim is to do the greatest amount of good, I do feel that the Saviour will make the gift a useful one. . . .

"The weather has been very cold, — very cold indeed. I don't know what I should do to live on a prairie. . . . Just wait, dear Mrs. C., till our parsonages join, and then see if I am not a good neighbor; running in every moment of the day, at the very times you are the most busy, and have to wish 'she would stay at home.'"

To the same lady, Jan. 7, 1867, she writes: —

"I am so glad your husband was pleased with the books, — dear, good man. If I could only give him a

fine church, parsonage, and five thousand dollars a year, that would be
worth thanking me for. But I want
to be remembered in his prayers. I
long to become like Jesus ; and, as
I remember that the prayers of the
righteous avail much with God, I
shall be a million-fold repaid if he
will take me with him sometimes to
the throne of grace, and ask the blessed Saviour to make me every thing
needed in my future work.

"What very cold weather you must
have, — the thermometer two degrees
above zero! I should think those
prairie hens, so famed there, and so
exceedingly delicate here, would be
frozen to death. How I would love
to see a prairie! I cannot imagine
one. Sometimes I picture out an

immense, barren plain, perfectly covered with hens and chickens; and then, out of pity for the poor creatures with no roost, I have to lay out a number of forest trees, and a comfortable rail fence. . . .

"Dear father is just as much interested in the prophecies as ever. I could not begin to tell you the number of pamphlets and books he has upon pre-millenarianism. They have each a different name ; and yet the contents seem so much the same that I should think one person had written them all. One drawer in his desk looks positively frightful. As you open it, enormous headings stare into your face, and on the cover of one is the funniest picture, representing the great battle. There are Turks rush-

ing across the desert on foaming
steeds, and the greatest confusion
everywhere, brought out more boldly
by a threatening sky. I had to laugh,
and father laughed too, at the idea of
representing such a scene. . . . I do
not mean any thing wrong: I believe
most certainly what father believes,
but I am content to rest *there*. I really
am perplexed when I read so many
persons' opinions.

"I think if we love our Saviour
with all our heart, and try faithfully
to serve him, if we hold the things
of earth very slightly, and 'have our
conversation in heaven, from whence
also we look for His appearing,' it
ought not to trouble us *when* He shall
come. All Jesus asks is to have us
ready to meet Him.

"And besides, this way of bringing the 'time, times, and half a time' near makes me feel I will not buy any more things than I absolutely need, and so I put off and put off getting what I want, going round the house dressed like a Randall's-islander. Then when John comes home I look at him with great, wistful eyes, and think, . . . I do want to be your wife, how I would love to work with you in the ministry; but that drawer full of books and that alarming battle-scene knock away my delightful hope, and I have to give a long sigh."

A few months later, to the same lady, she writes: —

"I was perfectly delighted with your last letter, telling me about the

parsonage, and looking at the con-
templated plan. The only sadness I
felt after reading it was that I could
not be Mrs. George Peabody for an
hour, and give you the required sum,
and a great deal more."

To a sister at school, January 10,
1867, she playfully says: —

"*Georgie* is getting along finely in
his lessons. As for geology, he can
tell just how old all the dirt is in the
garden, and what age it flourished in.
Our gravel appeared first in the Ston-
crean age, and the catnip-bushes at-
tained their greatest grandeur in the
Cataluvian age, just before man came."

And again, on the 17th, —

. . . "Hasn't this been a very wild
day? I wish you could see the Park.
It has drifted in great piles, looking

6

like hills of snow. Father says he does not remember such a storm since he was a boy."

Under date of March 11, 1867, she thus urges the same sister, in whose spiritual welfare she took a very warm interest, to make a profession of Christ before men: —

" I know the dear Saviour loves you, and has given you His Spirit. And now, dear sister, would you not love to confess Him before every one? Father and mother are sure you love them, but they are pleased when you tell them so; and don't you believe the blessed Saviour would love to have you tell Him? . . . When you think of what He did for you, won't you do the one thing He wants most of all, — confess Him before men? . . .

Think of the reward Jesus promises, 'They shall be mine in that day when I make up my Jewels.' Think of Christ owning you then, telling His Father and all the angels you are His.

"Our communion is the second Sunday in April. I thought you would be at home then, and perhaps you might be willing to unite with the Church. Don't mind if your poor little heart beats fast as you think of it. Christ will be with you.

"Do not be afraid that you may not live consistently afterwards. Just trust Jesus, darling. He has promised to help you; and those who have once belonged to Christ, He says no one is able to pluck out of His hand.

· · · "No one knows, dear sister, what I have written, — no one but

Jesus. Won't you honor Jesus and own Him at the next communion? I will strengthen you all I can. I will go with you before the Session, and that, you know, is composed in our church of only the minister and two elders, and I will stand by you when you confess His name."

It is very pleasant to add, that her wishes in this matter were complied with by her sister, and the two, side by side, commemorated together the dying love of our Blessed Lord.

She adds the following words of encouragement a few days later (March 20th) : —

"Jesus will take the very best care of His own. Why, has He not promised that all things shall ' work together *for good* to them who love Him '?

For good! — just think. for good! —
trials, persecutions, suffering, all for
good. It doesn't seem hard to be a
Christian: why, I think it is the most
delightful kind of happiness, — you feel
so peaceful all the while. To be sure,
we must take up the cross; but what
is that to bear, when the Saviour
lightens the load by bearing it for us?
We must bear His yoke, but then the
yoke He puts upon us is lined with
love.

"I suppose when we get to Heaven
and receive the crown, we will not
think our cross was too heavy then.
It seems to me that we will wish we
had done a great deal more for Jesus,
that we might feel more worthy of
enjoying the beautiful things He re-
serves for them that love Him."

A few months later she writes to the same sister.—

" Just try to please Him, dear; never mind what others think of you. Jesus will make you exert a good influence over them, though you may not see the effects. And if you never see it on earth, think how sweet it may be in Heaven when Jesus shall tell you of some one who might not have been there had it not been for you."

She kept a journal, beginning May 20, 1867. She made entries in it with considerable regularity through 1867 and '8. It was omitted during 1869, but began again in 1870.

We regret that our space will only allow of a few brief extracts.

On May 24, 1867, is the following entry : —

"Had an invitation to attend an entertainment for the benefit of a Sunday school in Yonkers. Oh, how I long to go! I know I murmured because my tract distribution would prevent me.

"Prayed God to bless the distribution of my tracts before I went out with them. Every one received them kindly. I have not grown in grace to-day. I have been discontented with my life. Others seem to have so much enjoyment on this lovely day, and my work seemed such drudgery, I forgot I was doing my Father's work. I forgot the reward He promises, and yet I would rather forget that than lose the deeper motive of doing all from love to Jesus. Oh the yearnings and strivings to be like Jesus! and bitter, bitter, are the tears I shed over failures and disappointments. It is truly only in 'looking to Jesus' that I gain strength and hope to go on."

"MAY 30.

"I have done a great amount of copying to-day, but then that was General-Assembly matters for dear father. I didn't mind it a bit, for it is a perfect pleasure to do any thing for such a dear, good man; and I pray God that I may have every opportunity given me to help father, even if he never knows I did it."

"SABBATH, June 2.

"I felt very earnest speaking to the children at Sabbath school of the Sa-

viour's love. It seemed to me that I
could not let one child go home without making them tell me that they
did love Him. Oh I must have them
Christians! I must indeed pray more,
work more, and find opportunities to
speak to them directly about Jesus.
It must not be that these souls shall
be lost through my negligence."

"JULY 14.

"To me the communion was a very
joyful season, though I trembled when
I saw the bread coming towards me:
I felt so unworthy to touch it. But
the next moment I remembered that
Christ wanted me to come 'just as I
am,' and though I was doing nothing
for Him. I felt with Peter, 'Lord, Thou
knowest that I love Thee,' for I do

love Jesus with all my heart. I am willing to give up every thing, and will do any thing for His sake. All through the day I find myself saying, ' Lord, what wilt Thou have me do?' Use me in some way, any way, but, oh, let me feel You think me worthy to work for You! Let it be in little things, that no one sees but You; and may I expect no commendation from any one, satisfied if I feel within me love, joy, and peace, blessed fruits of the Spirit."

"July 25.

"My dear, dear Saviour, I am all Thine, — use me, — do with me as seemeth good to Thee: only draw me nearer, nearer."

"I had a sweet time in prayer. I
felt Jesus was with me, right by my
side. Oh, when I have such glimpses
of His beauty, His love, and His
tender mercy, I long to go right to
Him, and throw my arms round His
neck and stay there for ever! I cannot
believe I will ever want to leave Him
in heaven. It seems to me that
through all eternity I will want to be
kissing those dear hands and feet,
and cry over them to think how sweet
He was to die for me; but I know in
that land there will be no tears shed,
and yet it would be so sweet to have
Jesus wipe away mine with His own
hand. Dear, dear Jesus! Can I ever
love Him enough, or live so as to
glorify His name? Saviour, help me."

"Mrs. L. has instituted a female prayer-meeting. I feel timid, fearing I may have to take part; but I want to leave it *all* to God, and pray for strength when the time comes."

Three days later she writes thus of the first meeting: —

"I wish I could describe the meeting. Mrs. Y. conducted the exercises. First she made a prayer, then we sang the hymn, —

'How blest the tie that binds.'

Afterwards she asked Mrs. L. and Mrs. S. to pray. Oh, what beautiful prayers they both made! I listened astonished. I thought, God is surely helping them, and I know He will help me. I wondered how they could be so calm; but I saw when they

arose that their cheeks had bright red
spots on them, so I felt encouraged, if
I was called upon, to attempt it.
Mrs. Y., after reading some extracts
on the power of prayer, asked me,
would I pray. I said, 'I will try.'
I knelt down, and, glory to God, I did
pray. The words came: I did not
falter. All the way through I was
helped: the tears are coming while I
write; it was so good in God. Oh,
how I trembled! I felt my body
shaking from head to foot. When I
arose I felt I had passed through a
fiery trial; but, thanks be to God, I
gained the victory through Christ."

A lady who was one of the main
supports of this meeting speaks thus
of Kate's connection with it: —

"I knew and loved Kate best in

the little praying circle, where she so often met us for a year or longer before her marriage. We all were much impressed with the peculiar directness and simplicity of her petitions, and how naturally, with child-like trust, she talked with Jesus. It was usual for us there to speak for one another in prayer, and say *we* ask — give *us*. But often when Kate led our petitions, after one or two decorous sentences, in which she evidently felt oppressed by the presence of others, as she approached her Saviour, she would lose this consciousness, drop the formal 'Thee' and 'Thou,' and in her rapid, earnest way would talk as friend talks with friend: 'Dear, precious Jesus, keep always near my side, — yes, in my

heart,—and then I never can forget;
for You know I would not willingly
do wrong, my dearest Jesus.' Once
after her marriage she was with us,
and then I recall her as she joined in
the hymn, —

> ' Jesus, Lover of my soul.
>   Let me to Thy bosom fly :
> While the billows near me roll.
>   While the tempest still is high.'

Little could we think then that she
in her freshness and strength would
be the first of our circle to reach the
haven. Every one of us had seen
more of sorrow and toil than she.
One had spent long years as a missionary in a foreign land, — another
had labored a score of years in the
service of Christ at home,—and some
of us, though younger than these,

have long tried to fight the good fight, and have again and again been overshadowed by sorrows Christ has sent. Yet she was the nearest Jesus: her walk was close with Him; and He loved her so, He took her to Himself. Even as when on earth He wept for the friend He loved, and called him back to His companionship, so He longed for this sister who cherished her Saviour so fondly, and He took her home. *Jesus*, 'the sweetest word on mortal tongue,' was ever on her lips in prayer and praise; and *Jesus*, 'the sweetest word in seraph's song,' will be her joyful theme for ever."

III.

THE MINISTER'S WIFE.

7

ON the 17th June, 1868, Kate was married, at her father's residence, to the Rev. John Newton Freeman, the newly elected pastor of the First Presbyterian Church, at Peekskill, N.Y. The ceremony was performed by her pastor, the Rev. C. A. Stoddard; the Rev. John Howard Smith, of the Episcopal Church, offered the prayer. The ceremony was at one o'clock, on one of June's balmiest days. Audubon Park never looked more beautiful than it did that day; and the pleasant little company

assembled agreed that it was an aus-
picious beginning of her new life.

Anticipating this event, she writes
to the pastor's wife, in Illinois, from
whose letters we have already given
several extracts: —

" I look forward to my home at
Peekskill with a little trembling, because of my responsibilities as the
wife of the minister; and yet I am
very hopeful, because I take Christ
at His word and have Him to lean
upon. Isn't it the sweetest kind of
peace to trust Jesus? The darkest
trouble and heaviest care are nothing
when laid upon Him. I have found
lately that the moment I begin to
worry, if I go right to Jesus and
tell Him that I do not want to have
the thing trouble me, I feel instant

relief. . . . Lately I have been unhappy because my life seemed so inactive. I could do nothing for Jesus
without having a terrible headache or
feeling tired out. I do not feel sad
now, because I have been reading a
sweet piece which comforted me very
much. It says that it is just as much
work for Christ to remain inactive as
to be continually occupied; and very
often we glorify God more by suffering patiently and waiting quietly, than
when engaged in the work we love
to do. I feel now that I am willing
to do or be any thing Christ thinks
best."

And again, to the same lady, about
a month before the wedding: —

"Our home is looking lovely now,
the trees are leafing so beautifully;

but I am not one bit sad to leave
it. . . . I love the work in which my
life is to be spent. I love it with
all my soul. I want to consecrate
myself entirely to it. I pray to have
such a burning desire to save souls
that all other things shall appear of
little consequence. God knows I am
ignorant of the duties called for in
such a work, but I am willing to learn
them. . . . O Mrs. C., won't you and
your dear husband ask God to show
me the way clearly? I need, so much,
wisdom from above. . . . You must
put the little card enclosed in your
looking-glass. You will be sur-
prised to find how many a heart-
ache it will save you. Indeed,
looking up does bring down the
blessing."

This card read, — " If you want to
be miserable, look within. If you
want to be distracted, look around.
If you want to be happy, look to
Christ."

While somewhat anxious about
the new duties so soon to devolve
upon her as a minister's wife, she de-
rived great comfort from attending
Rev. Dr. John Hall's Bible class one
Saturday afternoon, when in New
York. His subject was the call of
Moses to be the deliverer of Israel
from Egyptian bondage, and his
doubts and difficulties in view of that
great work. The good doctor little
thought, as he discoursed in his practical and earnest way, applying Moses' difficulties to those in every-day
life, that he was comforting one of

the Lord's children, unknown to him, but well known to the loving Master whom both served, — outside, it is true, of the doctor's own flock, but included in that greater fold of which Jesus himself is the Shepherd.

Instead of going away on a marriage trip, she preferred to go direct from her father's house to her new home and untried labor at Peekskill. The house was all furnished, ready for their use, by her parents, so they had only to enter and occupy. It was full of beautiful things, and was kept by the young housekeeper with scrupulous neatness and order. Though the Lord called her so suddenly and unexpectedly from us, yet after her death her things were found as perfectly arranged, every article as neatly folded, as if she had anticipated her sudden removal, and had made every arrangement accordingly.

In a letter of consolation to a dear friend bereaved of an only child, she writes, —

" Though you may look up through blinding tears, I know you say from the depth of your heart, ' It is well.' May God bring you out from this trial more holy, more into His likeness! and you know a Father's hand will one day wipe away all tears, and a Father's home will re-unite all parted ones."

To her western correspondent, April 19, 1869, she writes from Peekskill : —

" Father and mother spent a Sunday with us about three weeks ago. Father spoke for a Sabbath school here in the afternoon, and afterwards occupied Mr. Freeman's pulpit, giving us a grand explanation of the Parable of the Laborers in the Vineyard. Oh, how I enjoyed it, it was so like the old home days; and you may be sure if it was right I was proud of my father. In the evening father spoke by invitation in the New-School church. It was just as interesting as the afternoon service. I do think he is a wonderful man."

To her mother she writes, February 4, 1869: —

" It was so pleasant to have a letter from you last night! I had not expected you to write to me this week; so it was a double surprise.

It does seem a long time since I was at home, because I had no visit with *you*. I must come soon again, so that we can have one of our old-fashioned talks together. So E. has returned: I am real glad that she is better. When the weather gets milder I would love to have her visit me, but I will not urge her to come while the stoves are up, as we shall find it very *expensive* to keep her warm.

" To-night we have the congregational meeting to see about the Parsonage. Of course I am going to be on hand to propose lots of closets and very few stairs. . . . On all the fences in town there are large bills posted, with the most brilliant pictures, and enormous letters telling of some grand performance in one of our public halls.

Of course I know all's not gold that glitters; but I do want to go: you know I always was more fond of Barnum's and Van Amburgh's, than the other children, — yet I can't do it. Now if I was only a foundry-man or the fish-boy, what bliss! By and by some old, worn-out speaker will come here to lecture upon the 'manifest proclivities and inherent infirmities, as evinced by the practical evolutions in physical chemistry:' then John and I can buy a ticket. Oh, what pleasure to look forward to!"

To her correspondent in Illinois she writes: —

"There is a young girl's prayer-meeting connected with our church, which was commenced this year. At our first meeting we were a little com-

pany of three, now we number four-
teen: of this number only five are
Christians. I do pray God that all
may be brought to love the Saviour.
We meet every Thursday afternoon
at three o'clock. Will you sometimes
remember us then in prayer?"

About this meeting she writes to
a young lady in Peekskill, one of its
most active supporters: —

"God is gradually increasing our
numbers, and we must labor and pray,
believing that He will make us,
through the Spirit's guiding, the
means of bringing all our little band
to the Saviour. Yes, dear T., God has
used just such unworthy means before.
He will do it now if we only do all
we can, praying for His blessing to
follow every word and act done for

His glory, or to influence one soul to come out boldly for Christ.

"And let me tell you a plan (just between us two). I thought of it lately, and I feel it is the only way to make an effort direct and effectual. Will you choose out from among your friends *one* upon whom you will bestow special labor; that is, pray more for; seek an opportunity to drop a word for Christ, — always praying, with dependence on the Spirit, that God will treasure it up in her breast? I, too, have chosen one. We need never tell one another: but, dear T., if we are faithful, prayerful, and hopefully patient, one glad Communion day will reveal to one another that our prayer has been answered."

The girl that Kate selected in

conformity with the above plan was
P. H., one who had no love for God in
her heart. Not content with praying
for her, she strove also to bring her
into this little meeting. This was a
work of some difficulty, but was
finally accomplished. The next step
was to gain her attendance at the
Church prayer-meeting. P. H. finally
consented to this, on the condition that
she might go with Kate. Every
Wednesday night thereafter she was
promptly at the Parsonage, ready to
accompany the young pastor's wife
to the meeting.

How earnestly dear Kate both
labored and prayed that God would
give her this " one soul " is seen in
her diary and letters. At last, with
great satisfaction, she makes the following record, —

"I had a talk with P. H. after the prayer-meeting. Thank God she does love the Saviour, and is willing to confess Him. Oh! I must pray for her. It is all Christ: I can do nothing; Christ must be all in all."

Kate was spared to sit down at the Table of the Lord with this dear one whom the Lord had given her; and it was one of the most delightful events of her life.

It is pleasant to add that P. H. has been the means of bringing four others into this afternoon prayer-meeting, and is herself one of its staunchest supporters.

On Thursday, April 29, 1869, at 3 o'clock in the morning, Kate was taken with convulsions, which continued, with brief interruptions, till

eleven o'clock that evening. Many
days of weakness and unconscious-
ness followed, during which she was
watched over by ladies of the congregation with as much fondness, tenderness, and loving care, as if she
had been sister to them all. For
weeks her life was despaired of; but
finally, in answer to many prayers,
she was raised up again to compara-
tive health.

As soon as she was able to travel,
she spent a month, with her husband,
in her father's house, at Audubon
Park (July) ; and the next one at
Greenport, L.I., hoping to derive benefit from the sea air.

One of her sisters who was with
her at Greenport, furnishes the following incidents: —

The washerwoman whom they employed had two little children. They were always sent with the clean clothes. Every time they brought Kate's, she would take them into her room, and, after talking with them for a while, she would give each of them a picture-card and some candy.

An old man, going for his cows, passed the house morning and night. Kate always managed to see him, and say a few kind words as he passed; for she said it made him feel happy. Before she left he came to bid her good-by.

There was a little colored boy that she often met. She never failed to speak to him, and present him with a bright picture-card.

On Sabbath, if she saw any one

reading an irreligious book or paper, she would unobtrusively put some pleasing and attractive little books or tracts on the parlor-table.

There was a girl in the house who had been confined to bed eighteen years. Kate sent her every day a pretty little book or some flowers, and always accompanied them with loving words of sympathy.

In alluding to her severe illness, in a letter from Greenport to her eldest sister, she says: —

" I do feel very grateful to God for restoring me from such a sickness. I was almost in the border land, when He brought me back. I sometimes feel as if I had caught a glimpse of the new Jerusalem, and the shining ones at the gate. It was a lonely feeling I had when I came to consciousness and found the little stranger — the little daughter that I had longed for — gone. I used to be so happy: I never felt lonely, for I had that sweet hope, that delightful motive, to thank God for every moment. Now, when I see others with darling children, with just such tiny ones, I look up and ask, 'Was it necessary, Father.' I know it must have been; I know God did right, He always does. Yes: He has brought me nearer to Him; I love Him ten thousand times more; I trust Him more. . . . I do long to, — oh, I long to save souls; but I will be patient, remembering, —

'They also serve, who only stand and wait.'

And I am sure, this summer, God wants me to wait."

In another letter, from the same place, she says: —

"We attend the Presbyterian Church. They have had a precious revival, and are full to overflowing with the Spirit. The evening meetings are very impressive. Last night several spoke who were converted last winter. One was a sea-captain. It was very touching to hear him tell how the Spirit had striven with him; though in homely language, it brought tears into every one's eyes."

After her return to her own home, she writes to her father, Sept. 3, 1869: —

"I was feeling rather blue yesterday: you know the shady side of a minister's life comes sometimes, and after such a long vacation it is rather hard to commence work again. We have the dearest people you could find anywhere; but, like all people, there are always *some* who think the pastor and wife have nothing to do but to make calls; and this cannot well be done often, when you have over three hundred to visit. Don't think I don't love the good work; indeed. I would choose it right over again. I remember the 'servant cannot be above the Master;' all these troubles tell me that I am not a bastard, but a real son of God! I do thank God for sending them, as we are very apt to become indifferent to our growth in grace when all goes on prosperously. And after all, father, it is the way we take them: we ourselves either make them trials or blessings.

Well, as I said, I felt blue, and a real
old-fashioned homesick feeling, when
John came in and gave me a letter.
When I saw your picture, I just
looked at it and had a good cry. It
is so like you, — so like when you
don't exactly understand, and say, —
'Now, — now let me see. I haven't
got it straight. Just wait a minute;
who, when, where, what is it?' I
felt right at home again with all the
family, and in a little while I was a
great deal happier. I had to sleep
with you under the pillow, and the
first thing I did when I woke up was
to pull you out, and say, 'Good-morn-
ing.'

"I am so glad to have it. I do
believe I can work better with you
looking at me."

Her mother wrote to her every week. About these letters, she says, (Jan. 19, 1870): "I did have such a nice letter from you. O mother, your letters are such a delight to me, — so brimful of news. I do thank you over and over again for them."

At another time she writes: —

"Your splendid letter came to me yesterday. Oh, I was *so* glad to get it. I had no idea you were well enough to write, and when I saw it was really from you I was so happy. And it was so full of news. Nobody writes such a good letter as you do."

In a letter to her mother, dated Oct. 4, 1869, she thus alludes to the death of one of her most beloved parishioners, —

"I have lost my best friend, in Mrs. Nelson's death. Oh, how I miss her! Most every day I have a little cry to think I will not see her here again."

How little she then thought that in less than six months she would meet her in the abode of redeemed souls!

To one of her sisters she writes about the same time: —

"Be sure God has some work for you in your home, and *only you* can do it, and without you it will never be done. Remember, darling, that life is uncertain, time is short, and we must work for Christ *every day*. Never mind if you see no good coming from the word spoken: don't forget that God has said, ' *His word* shall not return unto Him void, it will accomplish that whereunto it was sent.' Not one good word then is lost; *remember that.* Don't be afraid, darling, to *speak* or *live* for Jesus. It will be worth all the struggle when He confesses us as *His children*, before His Father, at the last day."

To her mother she writes: —

DEC. 5, 1869.

"I don't feel as if my time was my own, as it used to be. We are the Lord's, consecrated to His work here. He has a great deal for us to do, and I know He will not bless us unless our first desire is to do His will. . . . Oh, I do love my home and people so dearly! As for our church, you know Dr. Hall's or Beecher's could not begin to compare with it."

The loving congregation were building a most beautiful parsonage for the young pastor and his wife. Many parts of it had been planned according to her excellent taste. She thus alludes to it, Dec. 10, in a letter to her mother: —

" Our house is going up like magic. It is surprising to see it grow. The frame is all up, and now they are laying the boards on the outside. All day I hear the hammering, and it is a very pleasant sound to me."

It was not quite finished at the time of her death.

To her brother-in-law she writes: —

DEC. 10, 1869.

" I want you to select some books that you think profitable for John, as helps to study: some that are newer, and that he would not be apt to have. And one I would like to be the 'Life of Brainard.'

"You know John is away; and I thought if you could send them to the house before Tuesday night I can put them aside, and he will not know about it till Christmas morning. I feel a perfect confidence in your judgment, so don't be afraid of not pleasing me. I promise at the outset to be pleased. . . . Oh, how I would love to give everybody something!"

On the reception of the parcel, she thus playfully writes (Dec. 13) : —

"The splendid-looking bundle has come, written over so grandly that I feel as if I must be Lady Mary Wortley Montague, or Madame Guyon, receiving Fénélon's confessions. You

see I don't have often such a huge
package addressed to the Rev. Mrs.,
so it is no wonder my head is a little
turned. . . . I know the books will be
just what John wants. I *feel sure of
it.* Indeed, I almost think he must
have been praying for them."

And to the same, in another letter
of about the same date, she writes : —

" How differently we grasp the
promises oftentimes! It seems easy
to believe for others, but so hard to
believe for ourselves. When we see
others succeeding in a good work,
we think God has made them for
that work, — we never could do it.
Alas! we forget that ' to him that
hath shall be given, and more abundantly.' We do not try our feeble
strength in the service of Christ, and,

waiting for more, lose so many precious opportunities perhaps never again to be recalled. If we would only do our little every day for Christ, and leave all the rest to him, wouldn't our homes be full of the Spirit and some parts of our land brighter because of our short stay here?"

On the 1st of January, 1870, she resumes her journal with the following entry:—

"Yes, I am going to commence again. It has been such a pleasure to read over the other two diaries (1867 and 1868), that I re-commence this one. I hope to keep it up. My sickness all the fall and winter has prevented me from attempting any new thing. Perhaps now I will learn

to look away more from myself. I
long to advance in holiness. I love
to see my growth from year to year.
God grant that I may be led by His
Spirit to give Him all the glory."

JANUARY 4.

" A few of our good ladies met
with me to talk about our having a
prayer-meeting. We have decided
to commence it this Friday, at two
o'clock. May God guide, and be
present with us."

She was only permitted to attend
two of these meetings.

JANUARY 6.

" I feel as if I had lived a year since
I last wrote in my diary. This
morning I woke up about two o'clock,
feeling that I was suffocating. I told

John that I felt nervous over the prayer-meeting, feeling that I could not lead it. We talked two hours. May God bless my dear husband for the Christian advice he gave me. Oh, I see my whole life so plainly now! Yes: I have thought that things could not be done unless I did them, forgetting Christ must be and do all. I have given up my afternoon prayer-meetings now until after the little one comes. I feel that God is leading me to see that I must be nothing that He may have all the glory."

JANUARY 19.

" Oh, how precious was our evening prayer-meeting! Christ seemed very near us. I do long to have the power of Christ rest upon me. I know I want to be all His. Dear Jesus, in whatever way You think best, take away ALL of myself, and give me Thy *precious, precious* self."

On January 11, she writes to her little sister : —

"We had such a good time on Sunday. Saturday night ten children from the Howard Mission came here to Peekskill. We knew they were coming, so they were all provided for. I took two: the others were divided around. My two little girls were real sweet. They were a little bit afraid at first, but afterwards they jumped about the room *so* happy. They thought the organ was wonderful. I let them play on it. When they went to bed, they wanted to lock the door, they thought it would be such fun ; but I told them it was a great deal nicer to keep it open. They told me in the morning that they did *not sleep any all night*, because the wind blew so hard; but I guess they did. Sunday afternoon we had an immense meeting in our church. Everybody cried. There was a baby four months old, and two other children about three years old, a little girl of ten, and a boy of twelve to be given away. The baby was so sweet. It looked all around the church, and put its little hand up to the missionary's face, and never cried.

"All the little girls sang together, then my little girls sang alone. Afterwards they had a collection of $105.00. Wasn't that good?"

The following little hymn was

sung, and the air so impressed itself on Kate's mind that she was heard humming it to herself as she went about the house in the discharge of her duties: —

There's a land that is fairer than day,
    And by faith we can see it afar ;
For the Father waits over the way
    To prepare us a dwelling-place there.

Chorus. — In the sweet by and by we shall meet on
    that beautiful shore, &c.

We shall sing on that beautiful shore
    The melodious songs of the blest ;
And our spirits shall sorrow no more,
    Not a sigh for the blessing of rest.

In the sweet by and by we shall meet on that beau-
    tiful shore, &c.

To our bountiful Father above
    We will offer the tribute of praise,
For the glorious gift of His love,
    And the blessings that hallow our days.

In the sweet by and by we shall meet on that beau-
    tiful shore, &c.

She had a drawer in her bureau which she called " sinners' drawer," full of tracts and books, adapted to the thoughtless and careless, from which she distributed as she had opportunity.   Not till the last great day of account shall we know what fruit has sprung up from this good seed, watered with prayer.

The following extract from a letter, dated January 19, 1870, shows her loving sympathy for others, and her readiness to rejoice with those that do rejoice: —

" Oh, I am so glad dear sister has a little son, and is doing nicely! I have thought of her so much lately, and have always taken her with me to God in prayer ; and now the answer has come. Isn't it sweet? ... I didn't think I ever would be so delighted over another such event, but this morning I am smiling all over with real joy. . . . I cannot do any thing heartily to-day, I am so full of sister and the baby. Isn't God good? Oh, ought we not to love Him with all our hearts?"

Writing home a few days later, January 25th, she says: —

"What a splendid visit we did have from father. Such an evening! Oh, why did I not listen more when I was at home! Never did I realize so deeply before what a glorious expositor of Scripture he is (yes, I did too); but somehow I did feel it very strongly that evening. Listen to every thing that father says, dear sisters: remember that some day you cannot enjoy them so often.

"Dear father, may God reward him for the good he does others by communicating these precious truths. I pray God to bless him for the benefit he has conferred on me in making me love the Bible ten thousand times more."

The last two entries we give entire. They record a struggle and a victory, and are a fit close to the precious journal.

FEBRUARY 8.

"Such another terrible day of bitter rebellion and fightings within I pray God I may never experience again. Towards evening a flood of tears relieved me, and my Saviour's strength was made perfect in my weakness.

"*Poor Kate.* . . . BLESSED JESUS."

"But to-day I have been very happy. God has helped me to bear my cross for His sake, and I do want to have His will my will. I was greatly strengthened to do my morning duties."

Kate never fully recovered from the effects of her severe illness in April, 1869. The trouble seemed to linger in her system. But while there was much feebleness of body, all who saw her could not fail to note her remarkable growth in grace.

Whilst her letters and conversation lost none of that wit and vivacity so peculiar to her, yet with this there was an increased earnestness and devotion to the Master's work observed by all.

Her loving affection for the people among whom God had cast her lot as a minister's wife was very remarkable. She always said that she would never leave Peekskill.

From the sea-shore, where she had gone for the benefit of her health, in the prospect of returning home she writes, " I shall be so glad to be among my own people again." One of the last complete sentences she was ever heard to utter was, " God bless our church when I die."

From the 1st of March, she was subject to brief periods of great pain, accompanied by severe headache; but on Saturday (the 5th) these pains became much more violent as well as more frequent. That week there was read to her a very able and

eloquent article on affliction, in one
part of which the thought was beautifully brought out that trouble is but
the shadow of Jesus, so when we are
suffering we may be sure that He is
near. While she was enduring one
of these paroxysms of pain she said to
her husband. "Jesus must be very
near me now, for I feel His shadow
all over me." Then she continued,
"Jesus can take all this pain away, or,
what is just as good, give me grace to
bear it."

Well might we imagine her saying,
in the words of the poet, —

"So I am watching quietly
        Every day.
Whenever the sun shines brightly,
        I rise and say ;
  'Surely it is the shining of His face !'
And look unto the gates of His high place
        Beyond the sea ;

For I know He is coming shortly
    To summon me.
And when a shadow falls across the window
    Of my room,
Where I am working my appointed task,
I lift my head to watch the door, and ask
    If He is come ;
And the angel answers sweetly
    In my home :
Only a few more shadows,
    And He will come."

About three o'clock in the afternoon she was taken with convulsions, which continued every half-hour till seven the next morning.

About ten on the previous evening, amid these convulsions, the babe — little Kate — was born.

The last one of these spasms, on Sabbath morning about seven, was much more severe than any that had preceded it, and left her so entirely

prostrate that no hope was enter-
tained of her recovery. At one time
it was thought she would not live an
hour; but at three in the afternoon
she rallied wonderfully, and fond
hope, ever ready to spring up on the
slightest encouragement, again comforted us. She lingered in an unconscious state till Thursday, March
10, 1870, when congestion of the
lungs set in, and at two o'clock that
afternoon she went home to Jesus.

Again, as at her previous sickness,
ladies of the congregation waited
upon her night and day with the most
untiring devotion. May the Lord
abundantly reward them for their
labor of love.

And the little daughter, for whose
sake the mother gave her life, — the

little Kate, — may God's best blessing descend upon her! The mother's prayers, offered for her before she was born, will not be forgotten by our loving Lord. May she prove a blessing to all with whom she comes in contact here; and when life's restless voyage is over, join her loving mother whom she will never know till then, in the "Christian's Home in Glory."

The funeral was on Monday, March 14, at one o'clock.

An entire car-load of friends went from the city to attend it. A thin covering of snow was spread over the ground, but the sky was bright and beautiful. The members of the family and intimate friends gathered at the house, where a prayer was

offered by the Rev. L. N. Mudge, of
Yonkers, after which, the coffin, liter-
ally covered with flowers, was carried
over to the church by the elders.
There a great audience, even as many
as could find entrance, were already
assembled. A selection of Scripture
passages was read by the Rev. Mr.
Millard, of the Second Presbyterian
Church, and prayer offered by the
Rev. Wilson Phraner, of Sing Sing;
after which a discourse was delivered
by the Rev. C. A. Stoddard, her
former pastor, full extracts from
which will be found at the end of
this Memorial.

At the close of these exercises the
long procession wended its way to
the cemetery, where, in the blessed
hope of a joyful resurrection, we laid

all that was earthly of her we loved
so tenderly.

But dear Kate is not there : she
sleeps not in the new-made grave on
the hillside, — that only holds the
frail tenement of clay. She, a ran-
somed and glorified spirit, is now in
the home of the blessed, with the
dear Saviour whom she loved so well.

"That clime is not like this dull clime of ours ;
        All, all is brightness there ;
    A sweeter influence breathes around its flowers,
        And a far milder air.
    No calm below is like that calm above.
    No region here is like that realm of love ;
    Earth's softest spring ne'er shed so soft a light.
    Earth's brightest summer never shone so bright."

Think of her

    "Where the faded flowers shall freshen, —
        Freshen never more to fade ;
    Where the shaded sky shall brighten, —
        Brighten never more to shade ;

Where the sun-blaze never scorches ;
  Where the star-beams cease to chill ;
Where no tempest stirs the echoes
  Of the wood or wave or hill ;
Where the morn shall wake in gladness,
  And the moon the joy prolong,
Where the daylight dies in fragrance,
  'Mid the burst of holy song :
    Sister, we shall meet and rest
    'Mid the holy and the blest !"

IV.

EXTRACTS

FROM

REV. C. A. STODDARD'S SERMON AT THE FUNERAL.

10

"COULD I follow my feelings this afternoon, I should take my place among the special mourners who crave consolation and instruction on this sad occasion. For so efficient was the help, so faithful the labor, so cheering the words, and so hearty the sympathy in the time of my own sorrow, of our departed sister, that I cannot but feel that I have sustained a personal loss in her decease. But I stand here to-day to discharge a sacred trust, — to fulfil the request of one who never needed to

be asked twice by her pastor to do
any Christian or kindly work.

"This, my friends, is more than a
family affliction.   A large circle of
relatives mourn here to-day; this
church grieves for one whom they
quickly learned to love and prize; my
own church sorrows for the removal
from earth of one of its highly es-
teemed members;   little children,
whom she taught the way to Heaven,
are looking upward with tearful eyes,
with a sorrow in their hearts akin to
that which the disciples felt when
their Master was taken from them;
and in lonely dwellings, in tenement-
houses, in the homes of the poor, in
the hearts of the sick and feeble, there
is sincere grief for this sad event to-
day.

"But, blessed be God, we do not sorrow as those who have no hope. Our sister sleeps; she rests from her labors; she is for ever with the Lord, and her works do follow her. For her to live was Christ, for her to die was gain. Death, though it has separated her from us, has only brought her into closer union with Christ, — a union that can never be disturbed. Freed from the anxieties, the cares, the infirmities, the fears, the miseries of this uncertain earthly lot, relieved from sorrow, sin, and pain, she is with Christ, which is far better. Blessed and holy is her state of rest,— the prelude to a still more blessed and glorious reward, when Christ who is our life shall appear, and she shall appear with Him in glory. 'Eye hath not seen, nor ear heard, neither have entered into the heart of man the things which God hath prepared for them that love Him.'

"Our departed friend and sister was a child of the covenant. Given to God in early years, she was instructed thoroughly in the word of God, and daily commended to Him in prayer. She had that inestimable treasure, a Christian home training; and few, even of Christian homes, could compare with hers, where the word of God was made the theme of daily conversation, and the teachings of Christ were faithfully applied to common life.

"Added to these teachings was the potent influence of consistent Christian example. Religion was

made a joyous and desirable thing in
this household, and it is not wonderful that the Holy Spirit found ready
entrance into a prepared heart, and
led her early in life to ratify the con-
secration of parental piety and love
by her voluntary act. Precious, indeed, must be the reflection to these
bereaved parents, that their labors
and prayers for this beloved daughter
were so abundantly answered. No
regrets for undone duty ; no drops of
bitterness for unfaithfulness mingle
with the tears which nature sends to
relieve their aching hearts.

"She grew up in this happy, Christian home, developing a lovely and
vigorous Christian character. With
rare gifts of mind and graces of person and manner, she easily won and

retained the love and friendship of all who knew her.

" In her, wit and keen perception were admirably blended with tenderness and sympathy, so that her wit was never used to wound, nor her lively appreciation of character applied to ridicule or injure others. She could cheer the downcast, and bring smiles into gloomy faces ; and also weep with those who wept, and sympathize with the distressed.

" She possessed artistic talent in no mean degree, and many memorials of her taste and skill adorn the walls of her family and friends. To a thorough education she added a taste for valuable literature, and continually enriched her mind with the treasures which learning offers to the eager student.

" But all her gifts and talents were consecrated to Christ's service, and her special enjoyments were found in direct and personal labors for the Lord. Her Sabbath-school class loved her, because they knew, with the quick perception of youth, that she loved and labored for them with all her heart; the aged, the poor, and the distressed welcomed her visits, for they felt that she came in the spirit of her Master, and brought His blessing to their humble abodes, as well as food and clothing and comforts ; and the little circle of praying women, with whom she sought the mercy-seat, gladly followed her in that loving approach to a Saviour near and precious, which her prayers revealed.

"And when she went from her father's house to adorn and bless a new home, as the wife of a much loved man of God, prayers and benedictions followed her to this place. What she has been here, in the home now desolated by her death, in this church so deeply bereaved, and in this community so largely represented in this audience, most of you know full well.

"Her house was always attractive, and all were welcomed there. She entered with a lively interest into all the plans and labors of her husband for the spiritual welfare of this people, and exhibited the unselfishness which was a prominent feature of her character, in the cheerfulness with which she lightened his burdens,

and the assiduity with which she aid-
ed him to extend his influence and
follow up his ministrations.

" When, a year ago, she was
brought near to the gates of death,
her mind was stayed on God ; and
those who have seen her since have
marked a growth in holiness and likeness to Christ, which permits us to
apply to her the Saviour's beatitude,
' Blessed are the pure in heart, for
they shall see God.'

" To some it may seem a sad pri-
vation that during the last days of
her life she was unconscious ; but
dying words could add no witness to
the testimony of thy life, dear friend,
that all is well with thee. We will
not find fault with infinite wisdom
for taking thee away, nor for the

manner of thy departure ; but rather bring a tribute of gratitude to God, for such a life, and, placing it upon the coffin, humbly pray that the precious fragrance of thy example may be inbreathed by all these sorrowing relatives and friends.

"My brother in Christ, it has been my pleasure and privilege to know you in those intimate relations which bind hearts closely together, to counsel and to guide you, and to rejoice at your happiness, and increasing honor and usefulness as a minister of the Gospel ; and now 'I am distressed for thee, my brother.' The sympathy and prayer which you can claim are freely given ; but our best human efforts fall short of your great need. Therefore we commend you

to God, and to the word of His grace,
— that gracious word from which you
have often been able to draw consolation for afflicted members of your
flock. May the peace of God keep
your heart and mind through Jesus
Christ. May this bereavement be
a means of sanctifying you for the
duties of life, and of preparing you for
a blessed reunion with your departed
wife. This church that you have
instructed, counselled, and prayed
for, shares deeply in your grief, and
invokes the presence of the Holy
Comforter to heal your own and
their wounded hearts. May He come,
— the Messenger of Christ, — bringing to both pastor and people a blessing from the Man of Sorrows, which
shall make this affliction the means

of a far more exceeding and eternal weight of glory.

"We commend these parents and grandparents, brothers and sisters and friends, to the gracious Saviour. Oh, what sweet and soothing memories will brood, as on dove-like wings, over that home from which our sister, less than two years ago, went forth. As these recollections arise, may God make them divine ministers to point you all onward in the path of duty; and, as the little babe which God has kindly spared to bear the face and name of her departed mother, grows into womanhood (which God grant), may the Saviour print His Gospel on her heart, and make her such a servant of Christ as this mother was.

"If there are any here without a hope in Christ, and without experience of what it is to be a Christian, may God teach them the worth of such a hope in a time of affliction, and give them grace to learn from the character of our departed friend how to live as disciples of the Lord Jesus Christ."

" I go to life and not to death ;
    From darkness to life's native sky :
I go from sickness and from pain
    To health and immortality.

" For toil there comes the crowned rest ;
    Instead of burdens, eagle's wings ;
And I, even I, this life-long thirst
    Shall quench at everlasting springs.

" God lives ! Who says that I must die ?
    I cannot, while Jehovah liveth !
Christ lives ! I cannot die, but live ;
    He life to me for ever giveth.

" Let our farewell then be tearless,
    Since I bid farewell to tears ;
Write this day of my departure
    Festive in your coming years."
                       BONAR.

www.ingramcontent.com/pod-product-compliance
Lightning Source LLC
Chambersburg PA
CBHW030904050726
47500CB00009B/1016